Our *Flag* was Still There

OUR FLAG WAS STILL THERE

Published by
HIS SEASONS®
Copyright © 2004 Tracy Leininger.
All rights reserved.

Layout & Design by
Jason Roberts & Associates, Inc., San Antonio, Texas

Cover Illustration & Interior Illustrations by
Bill Farnsworth

No Portion of this book may be reproduced in any form
Without written permission from the publisher.

Printed in the United States of America by Jostens

ISBN 0-9724287-3-9

HIS SEASONS®

8122 Datapoint Drive
Suite 1000
San Antonio, TX 78229
(210) 490-2101
www.hisseasons.com

Our Flag Was Still There

The story of
The Star-Spangled Banner

―― To ――

Richard *"Little Bear"* Wheeler –

historian, evangelist and long-time family friend.

Thank you for making history come

alive for me in my early years.

Your unique, dramatic style and passion

for communicating our nation's

heritage has truly been an inspiration.

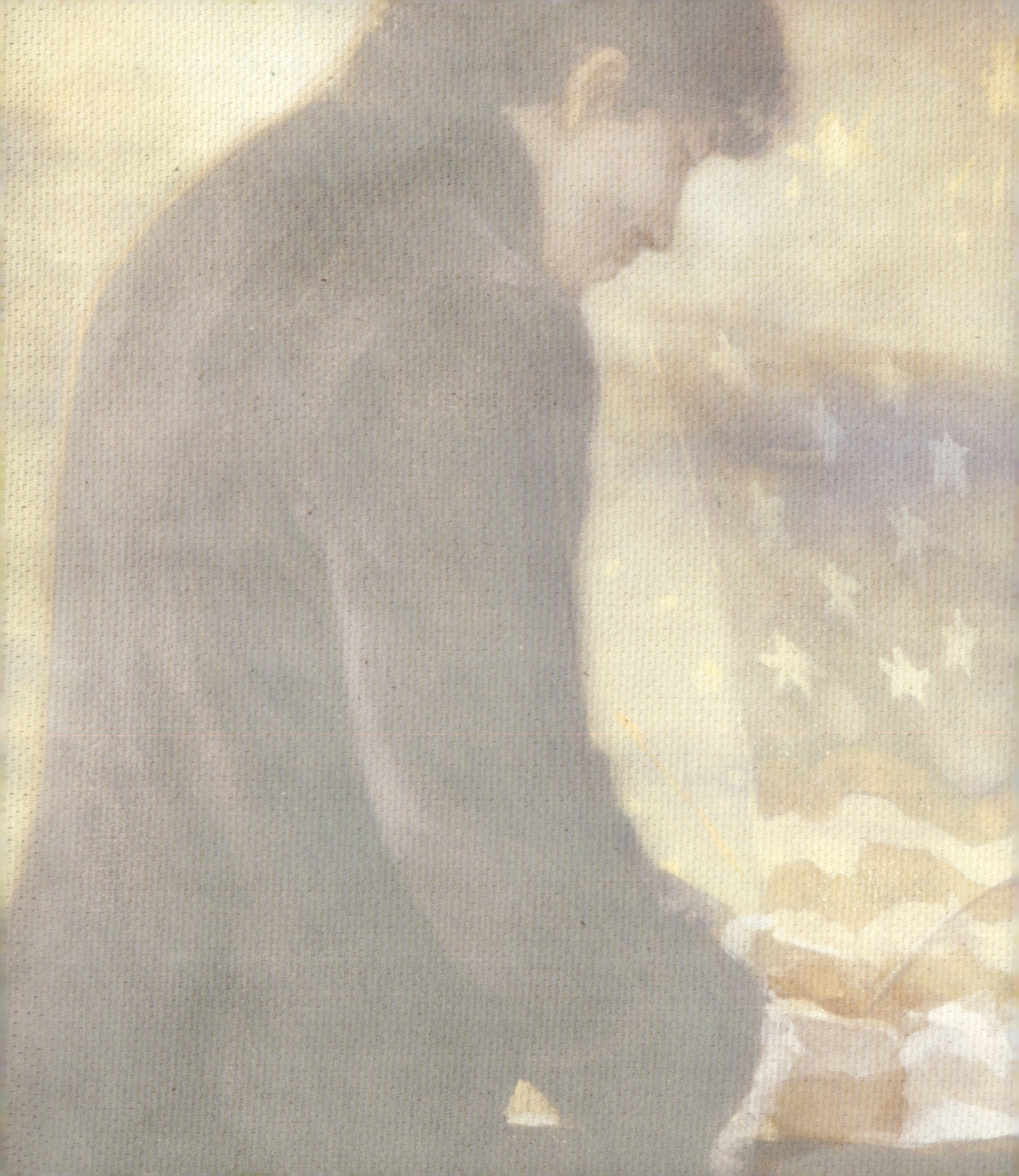

FOREWORD

As we approach the 60th anniversary of the Battle of Iwo Jima and the single most famous and inspiring photograph in history – the raising of the Stars and Stripes on Iwo's Mt. Surabachi – we are reminded of yet another day when the bullet ridden flag of free men was gloriously preserved by the kind and merciful hand of Providence. Who could have imagined that the heroic gallantry of a young lawyer in the face of foreign treachery on our soil would have resulted in the stirring words of a national anthem that has set an unsurpassed standard for all nations and all time.

When you consider the legacy of untold legions of heroic men who have died to preserve the freedoms symbolized by this great flag, or the more than a half a billion Americans who have heard, sung, and thrilled at the great Anthem to our flag penned by Francis Scott Key on that lonesome night on September 14, 1814, our mission seems clear – we must preserve this glorious heritage by sharing it with our children.

I simply can not imagine a more effective literary vehicle for sharing this God-blessed moment in history. With beauty and nobility, Tracy Leininger has given parents the ideal means to do just that. Bravo!

Doug Phillips
President, Vision Forum

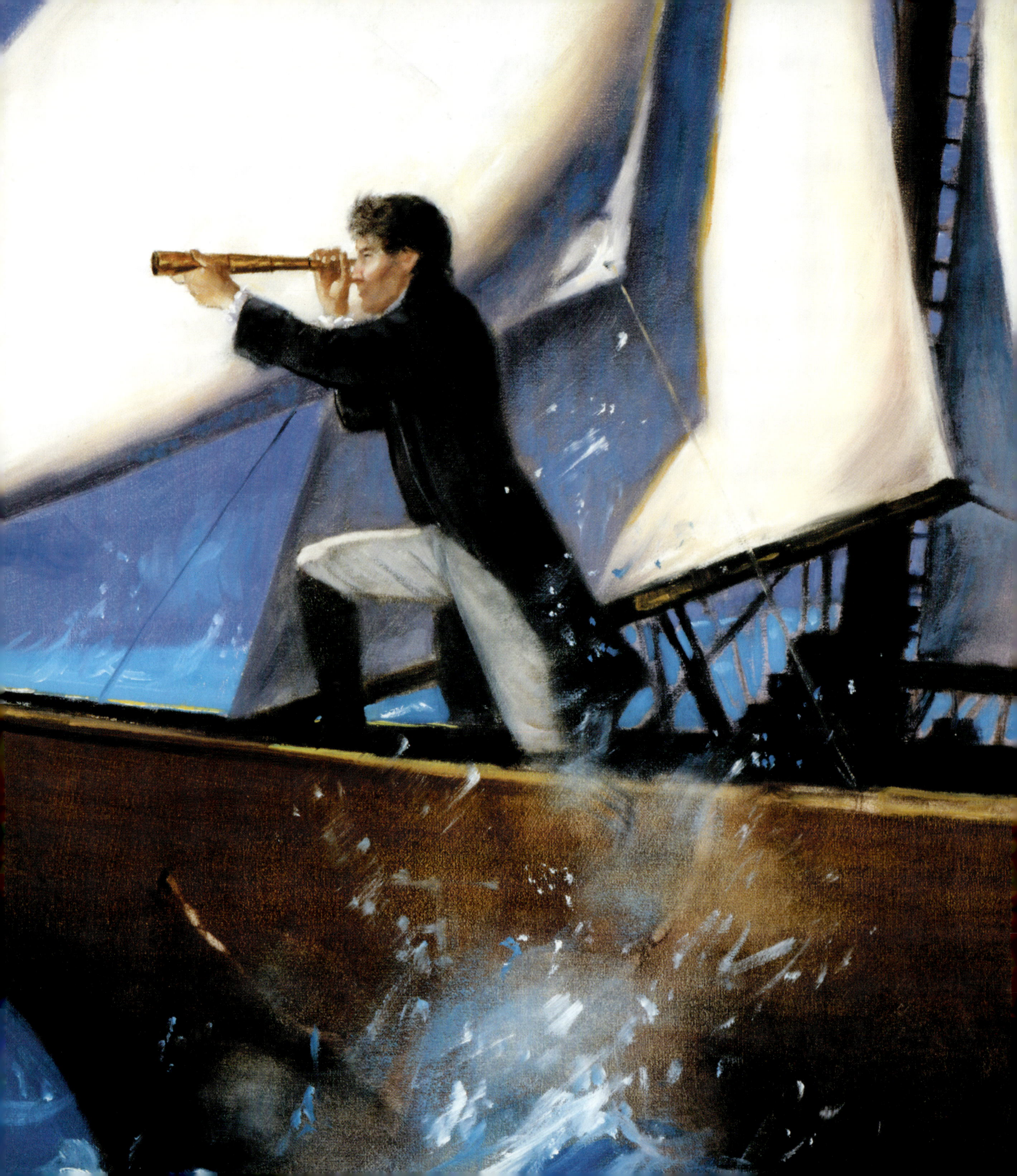

"British war ships straight ahead!" Francis Scott Key called from the bow of his small schooner. "Should we hoist the flag of truce now or wait until we are closer?"

"Now sir!" Colonel John Skinner answered. "We're at war and the sooner we let them know that we come in peace the better."

Chilling September winds ripped through the sails and wrestled with the white flag, which Colonel Skinner hastily tied to the flagpole. The waves pounded against their vessel, throwing salty spray high into the air.

Francis dried his spyglass, hoping to get a better look at the enemy fleet. *Will General Ross receive us or throw us in the brig?* he thought. *Where is the Tonnant, his command ship? Does it still hold captive the good Dr. Beanes?*

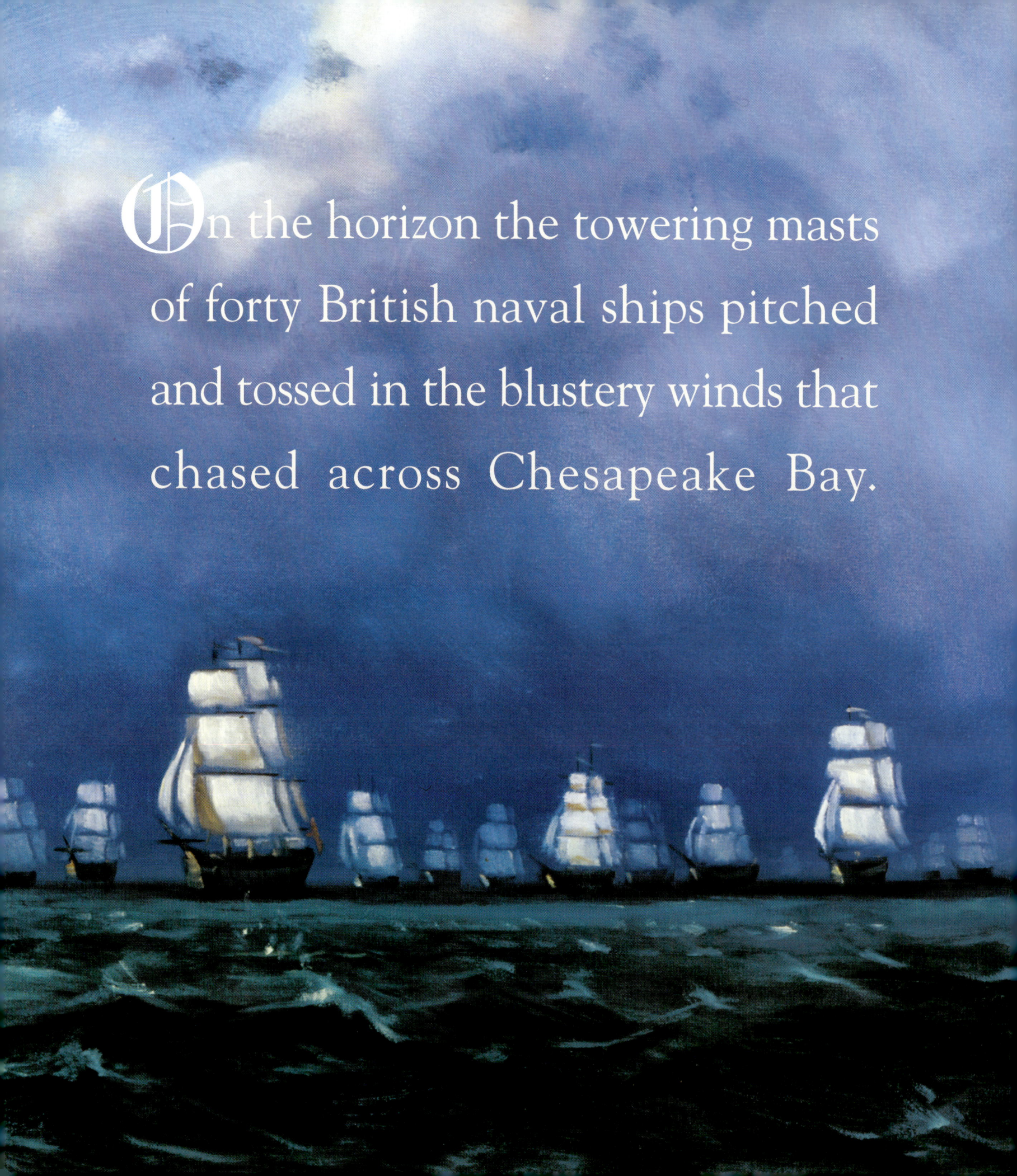

On the horizon the towering masts of forty British naval ships pitched and tossed in the blustery winds that chased across Chesapeake Bay.

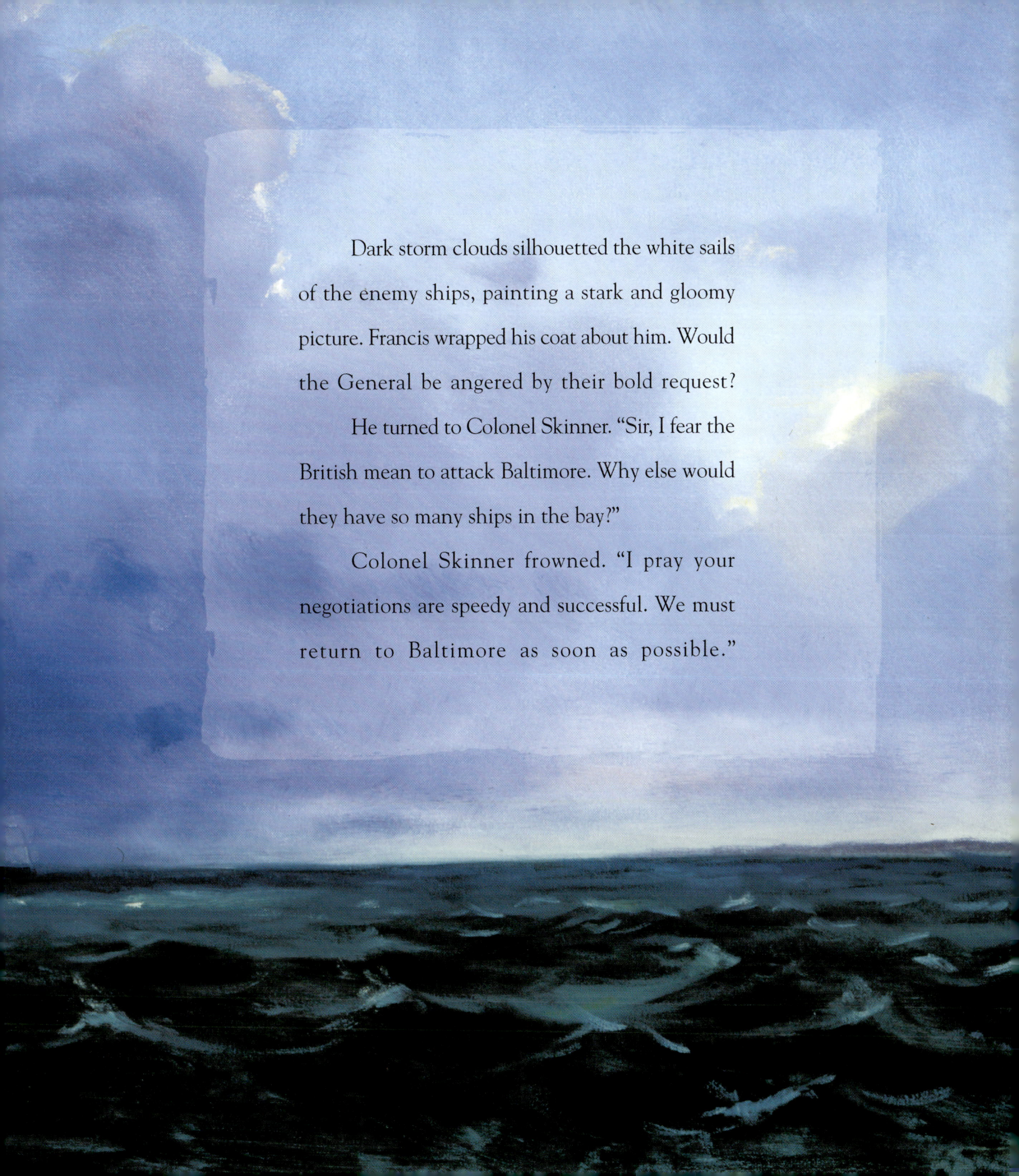

Dark storm clouds silhouetted the white sails of the enemy ships, painting a stark and gloomy picture. Francis wrapped his coat about him. Would the General be angered by their bold request?

He turned to Colonel Skinner. "Sir, I fear the British mean to attack Baltimore. Why else would they have so many ships in the bay?"

Colonel Skinner frowned. "I pray your negotiations are speedy and successful. We must return to Baltimore as soon as possible."

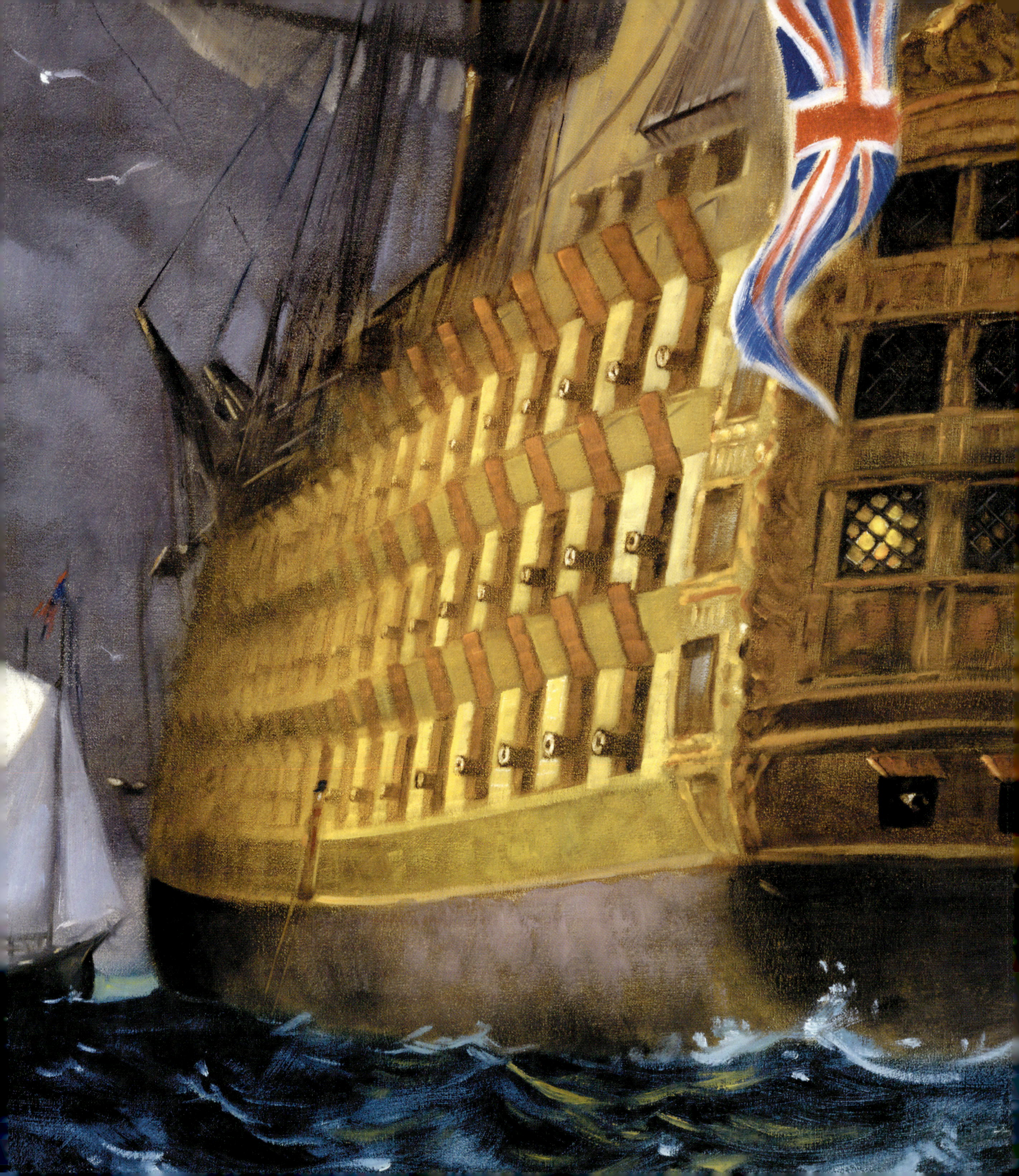

They neared the British fleet, which dwarfed their little sloop. Finally, they spotted the huge vessel *Tonnant*, bristling with cannons.

Francis looked up through the great rigging. "I'll not leave until the kind old Doctor is released," he said. His face sobered as he looked back across the water separating him from his homeland.

Upon boarding the *Tonnant*, they were ushered to the officers' quarters. It was easy to sense the arrogance and defiance of the British commanders. Francis knew his job would not be easy.

𝕭reathing a quick prayer, Francis introduced himself to General Ross. "Sir, I have been sent by President Madison to negotiate the release of Dr. Beanes."

General Ross laughed. "He is a traitor to England and will be treated as one."

"If you please, sir," Francis said, "I have letters written by the hands of your own soldiers attesting to the kind medical service the doctor rendered them." Francis handed the General the papers, hoping they might persuade him.

Negotiations continued for some time, and Francis began to fear the worst. But slowly, the General began to change his mind.

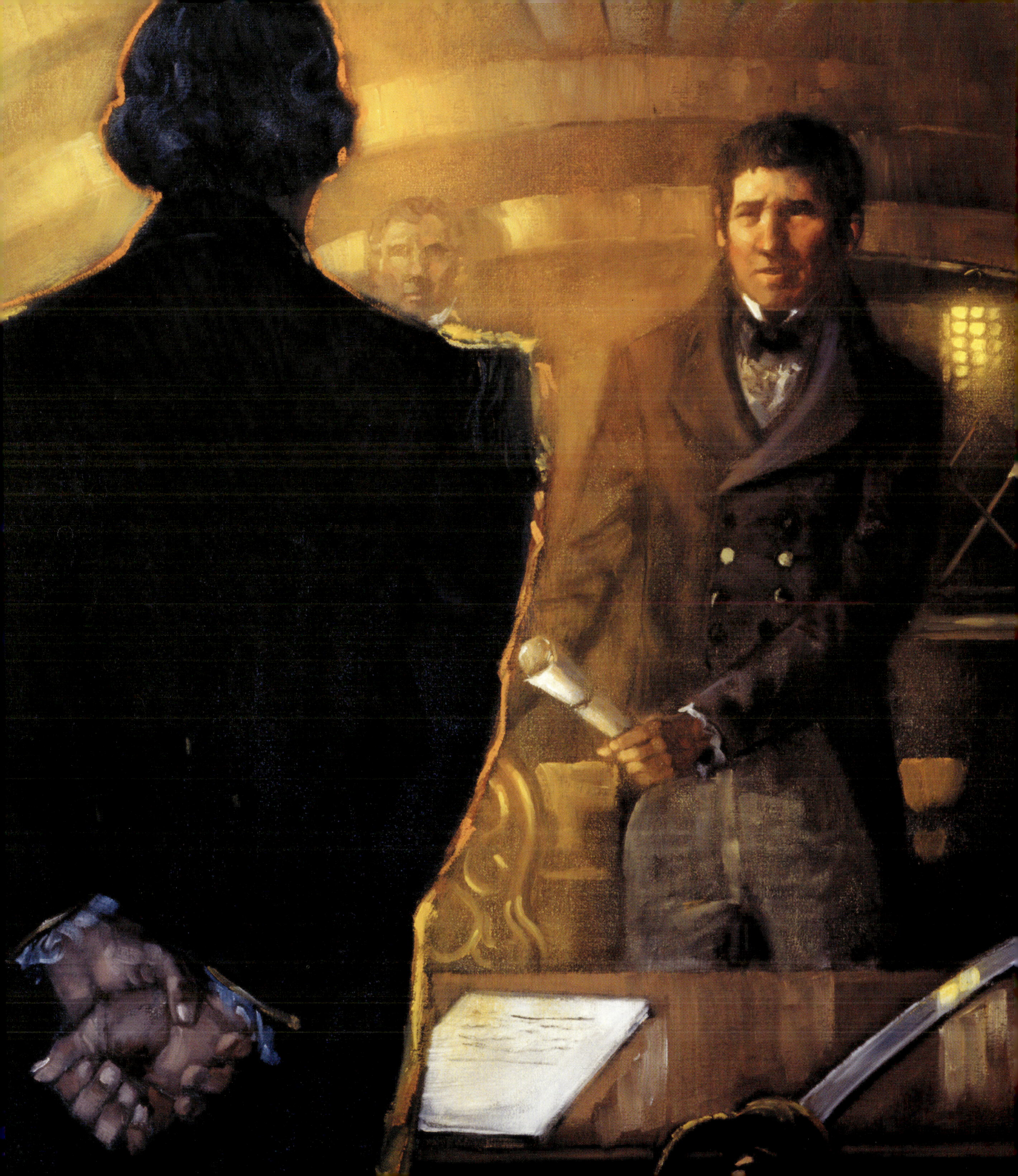

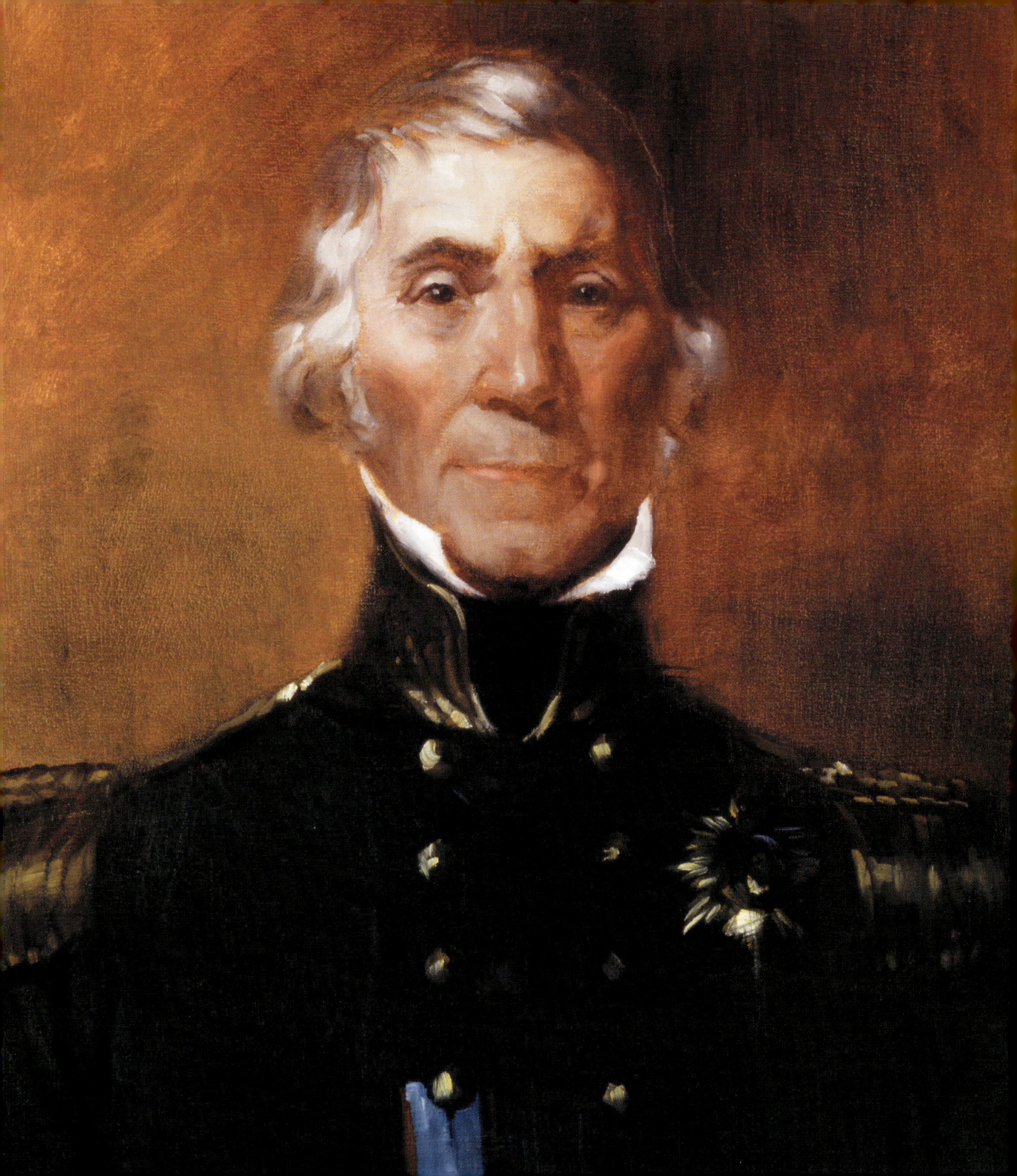

"Well, Mr. Key, they say that you are a convincing lawyer and rightfully so. I think we can come to an agreement so that you may have your Dr. Beanes back."

"Thank you, sir." Francis reached out his hand, but the General ignored it as he turned on his heel.

"However, you may not leave…not yet."

"Sir?" Francis asked.

"We plan to attack Fort McHenry. Soon you will see the power of the British Imperial Navy that you Yankee Doodles have so foolishly provoked. When Fort McHenry falls, we will march on to Baltimore." The General's eyes glowed with visions of victory and glory. "The men have been ordered to burn the city to the ground as we did in Washington. So Mr. Key and Colonel Skinner, there will not be much for you to return to."

Francis' pulse surged as he looked anxiously at Colonel Skinner. He remembered the battle of Bladensburg just weeks before. Francis had been a militia officer. His men were no match for the well-trained Imperial Army, and within hours the militia had sounded the retreat.

The British then marched into Washington and left the city blazing like a furnace. Francis remembered families running for their lives. Even his own wife and children had to flee their home in nearby Georgetown. That night the fiery glow of their beloved capitol could be seen all the way from Baltimore, Maryland. Now Baltimore seemed doomed to the same fate.

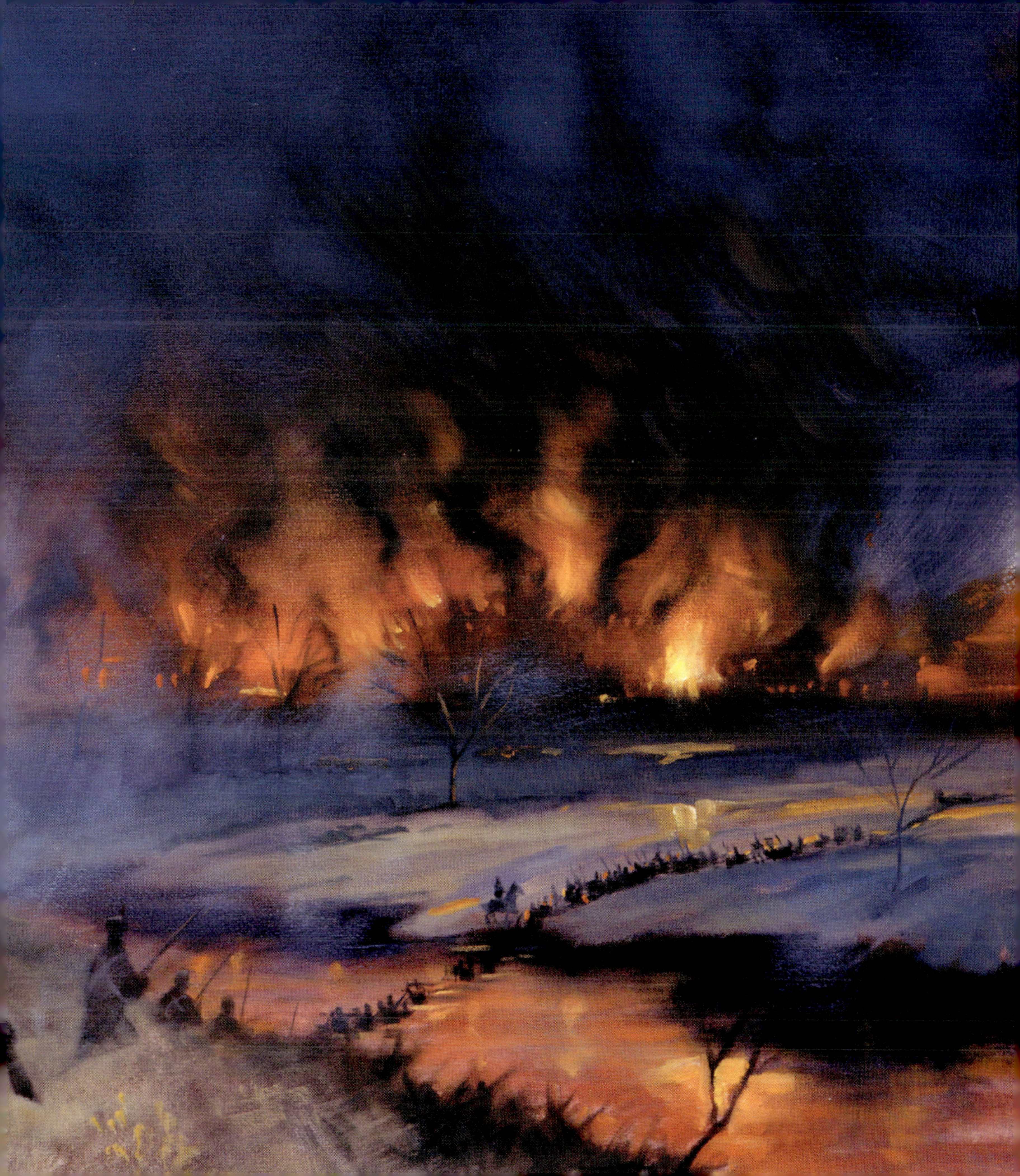

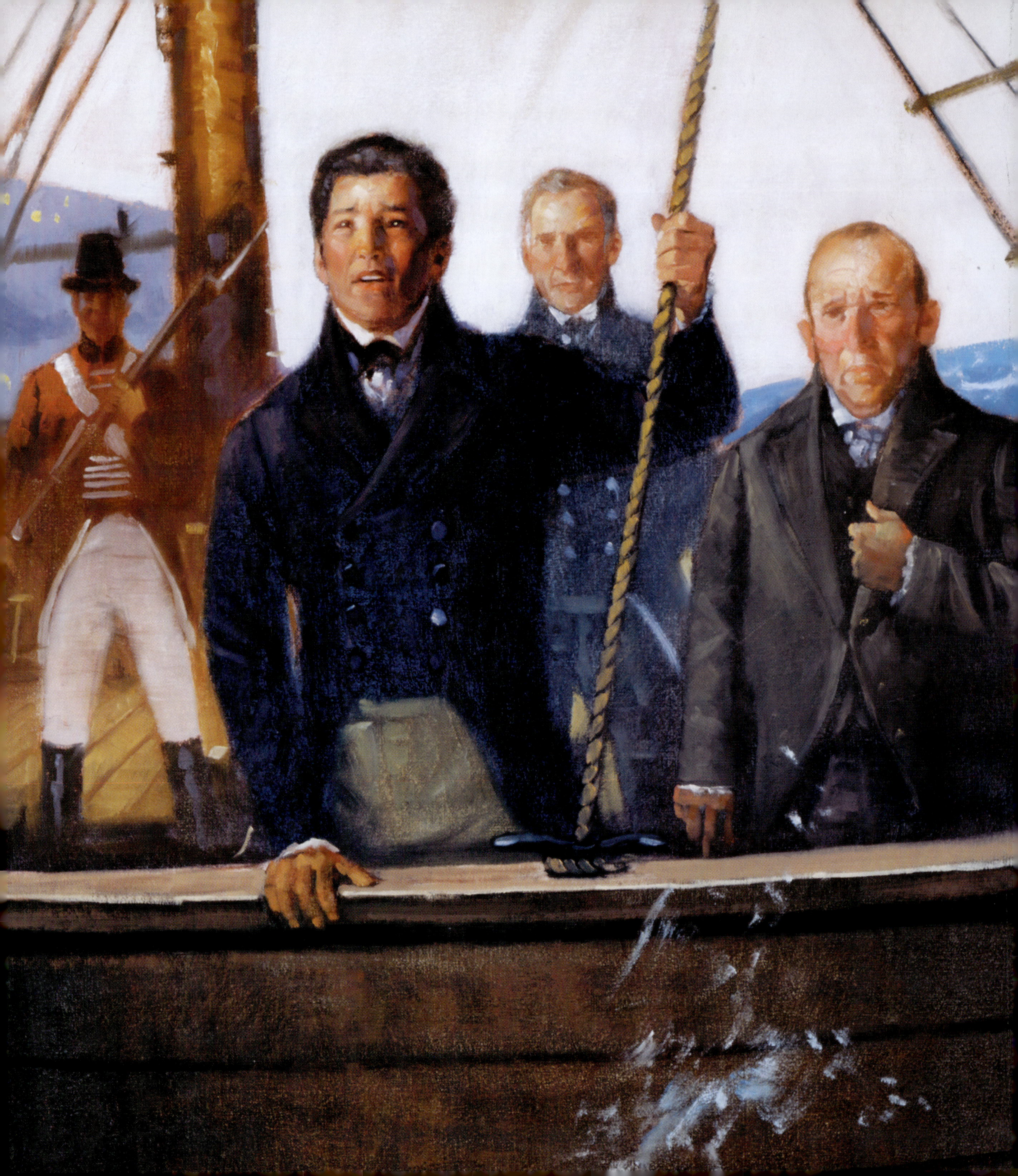

After being reunited with Dr. Beanes, the British officers escorted the party of Americans to one of their smaller war ships, the *Surprise*, led by the Admiral's son, Sir Thomas Cochrane. There they stayed for nearly a week. Though the British treated them with respect, Francis felt trapped and helpless. There was nothing he could do except wait and pray.

Finally Admiral Cochrane approached. "You are to return to your sloop immediately."

"Are we free to leave, sir?" Francis asked, jumping to his feet.

"No, that will be impossible. You'll be under the constant watch of our marine guards."

Soon the entire British fleet moved up the bay to the mouth of the river. The ships swayed to and fro as the sailors weighed anchor. Francis anxiously searched the shore through his spyglass. They were nearing Fort McHenry. He could see the American flag waving high and strong above the ramparts. Dr. Beanes, Colonel Skinner, and Francis Scott Key looked at the ominous line of nearly forty British war ships and then back in the direction of the fort.

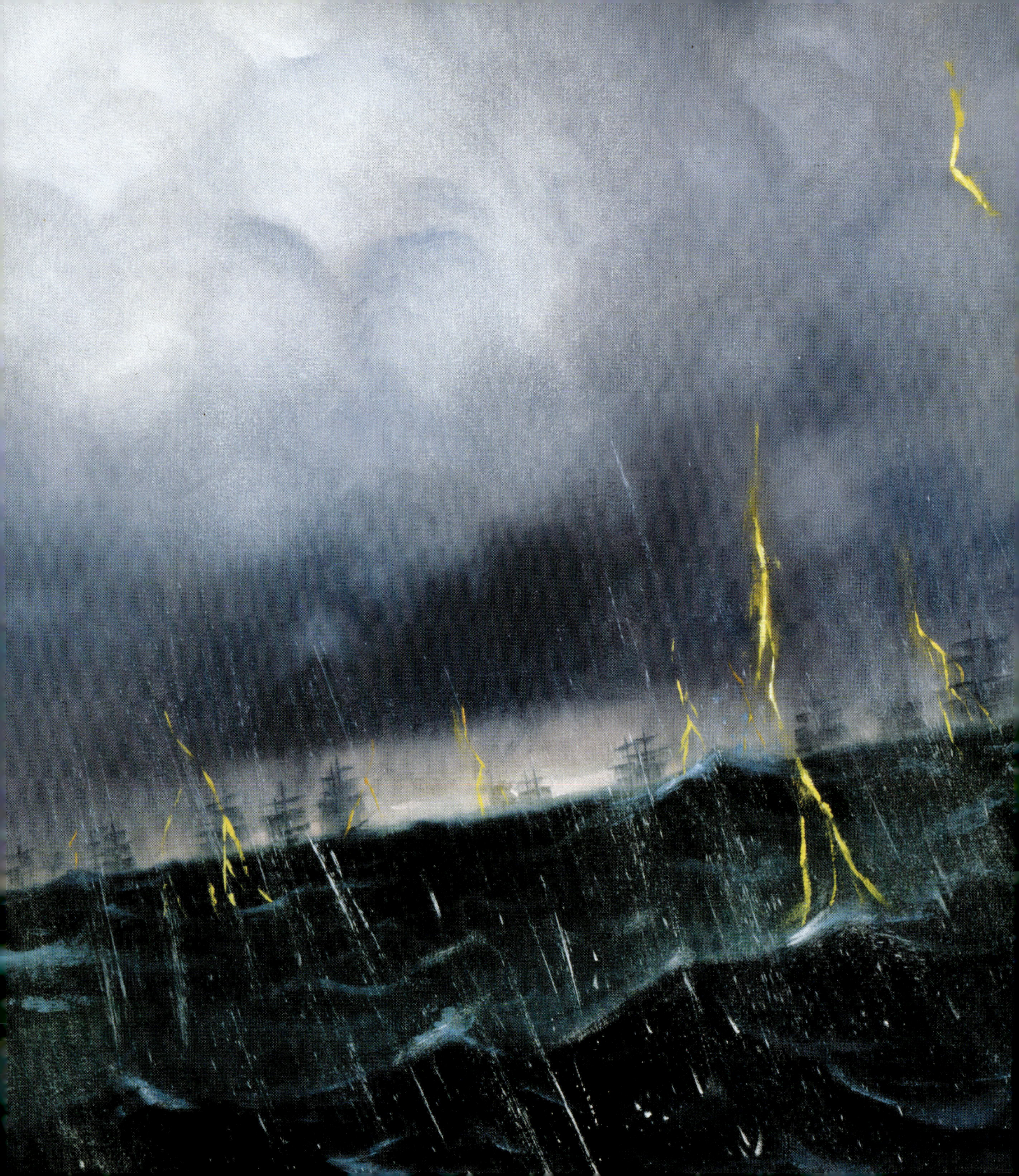

"Admiral Cochrane boasts that they can conquer the fort within hours and that looks to be true." Dr. Beanes' voice shook with emotion.

"Take heart, good man." Francis handed his spyglass to the doctor. "Look at our flag! She waves high and strong – a symbol of courage."

"His words are true, sir!" Colonel Skinner said. "As long as our flag still waves, Baltimore is free." A roar of thunder broke the silence. They had been so intently focused on Fort McHenry that they had not noticed the heavy storm clouds moving in behind them. Darkness soon hung about them, and torrents of rain fell in sheets.

"With this storm hastening nightfall," Colonel Skinner said, "I think we can safely say we will not see enemy fire tonight."

Early the next morning, Francis woke with a start. Had he heard a thunderous explosion or was it just a bad dream? Through the porthole, he caught sight of an intense ball of fire ripping its way through the darkness of the stormy sky. He leaped to his feet and rushed to the top deck. The British had opened fire on Fort McHenry. Another shot was fired. Francis grabbed his spyglass. The river in front of the fort exploded, shooting water high into the air.

"The rocket fell short!" he exclaimed. Another blast rang out across the river, followed by yet another. Francis' eyes grew wide in amazement. A soaring rocket flew so high that it pierced the giant American flag, robbing it of one bright star.

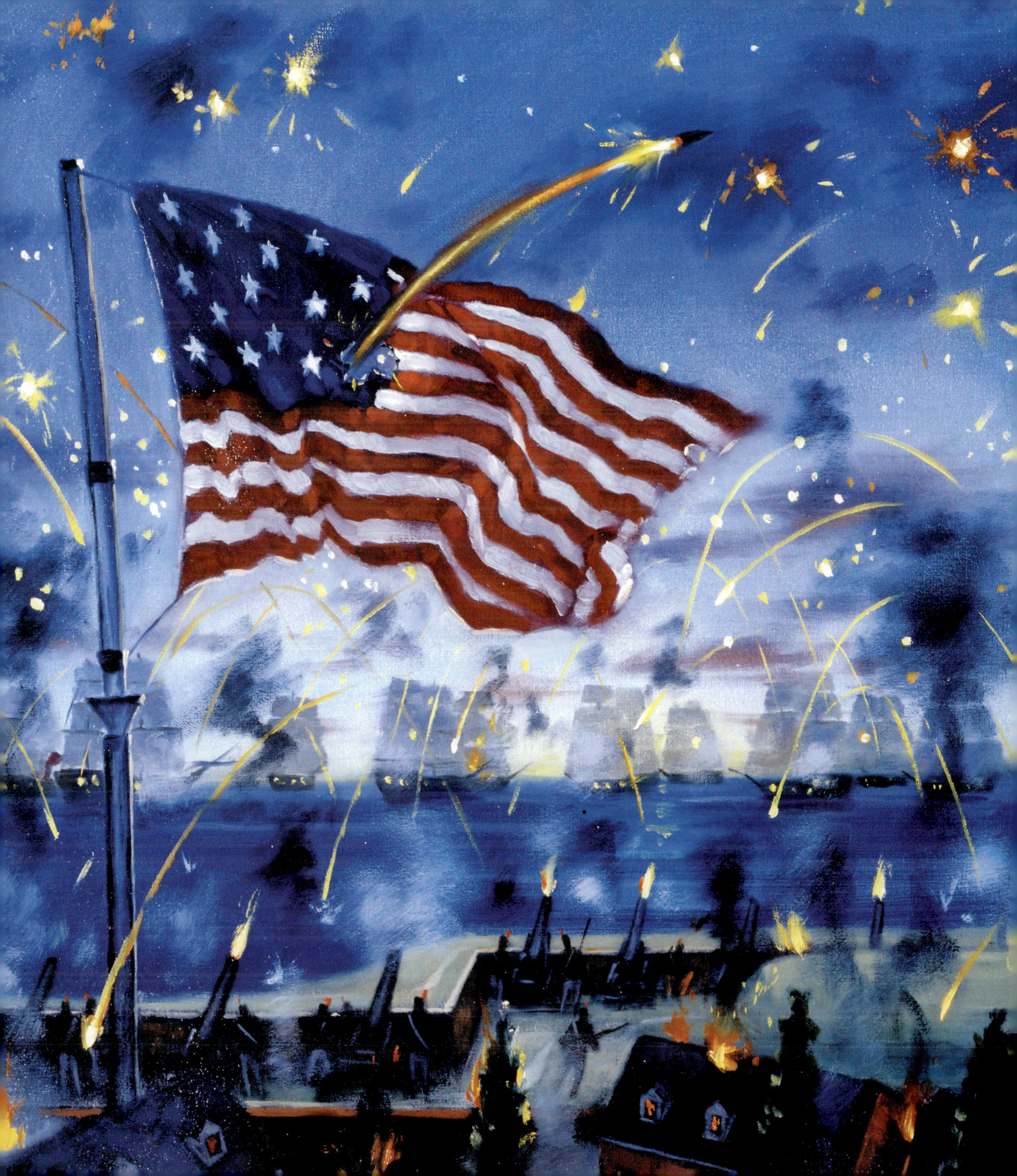

Cannons exploded until the boat rocked. Soon the morning light was darkened by smoke and fog. By now, Dr. Beanes and Colonel Skinner were also on deck.

They watched helplessly as rocket after rocket screamed through the sky toward their beloved homeland. The dismal rain continued to pour down on their heads. Still, Francis stayed on deck, watching for any sign of life from the fort. He cringed with each cannon blast.

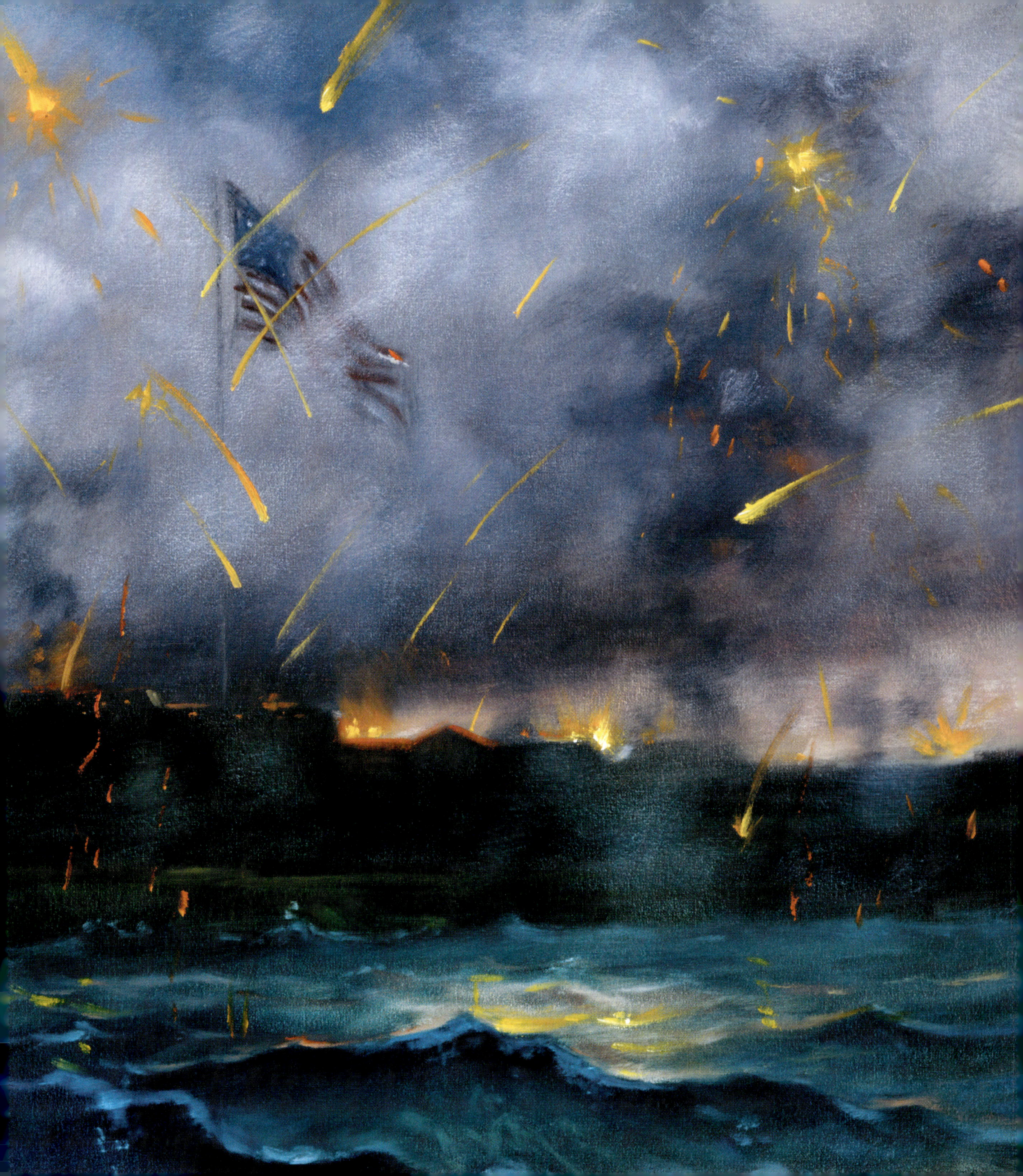

The hours passed slowly, but as the day came to a close, hope flourished within his heart. As the last rays of twilight reflected over the waters, he caught a glimpse of their great banner, cutting through the smoke and glare of the enemies' rockets.

"Look well on that flag," sneered one of the marine guards. "She won't be there in the morning."

Francis ignored the guard. The flag waved grandly over Fort McHenry as if to give a final salute to the day. He shook his head and muttered under his breath, "I admire her bravery, but how I fear for her safety."

His mind raced back to when he was a young boy growing up in Maryland on his family's plantation. He spent many happy hours playing on the banks of Pipe Creek. He remembered how in the evening their family would sit around the hearth and read or talk by the firelight. His father often told him stories of the battles he fought during the War of Independence.

"Son, never underestimate the price of freedom," his father would often say. "Remember, many good men gave their lives for the liberties you now enjoy."

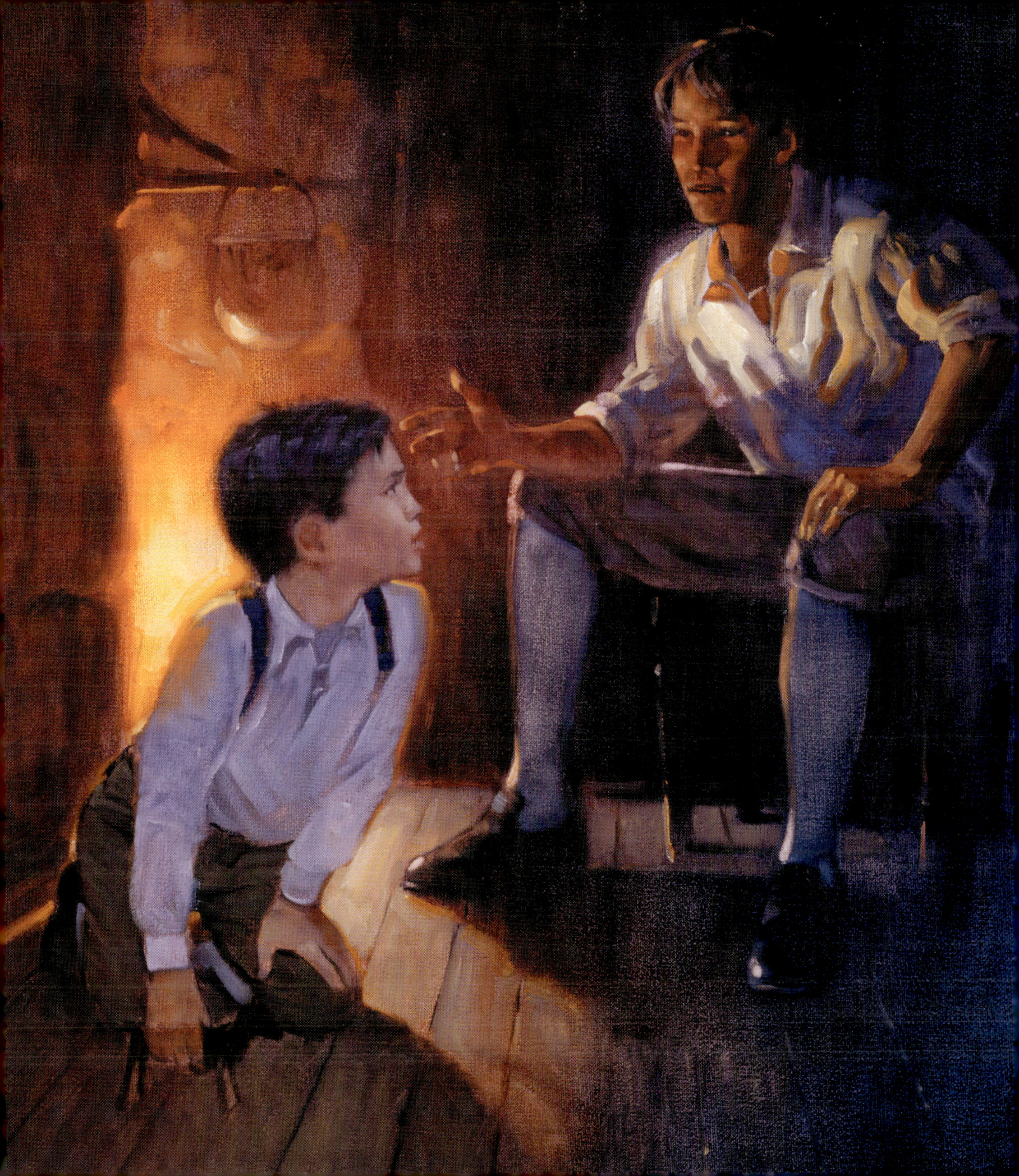

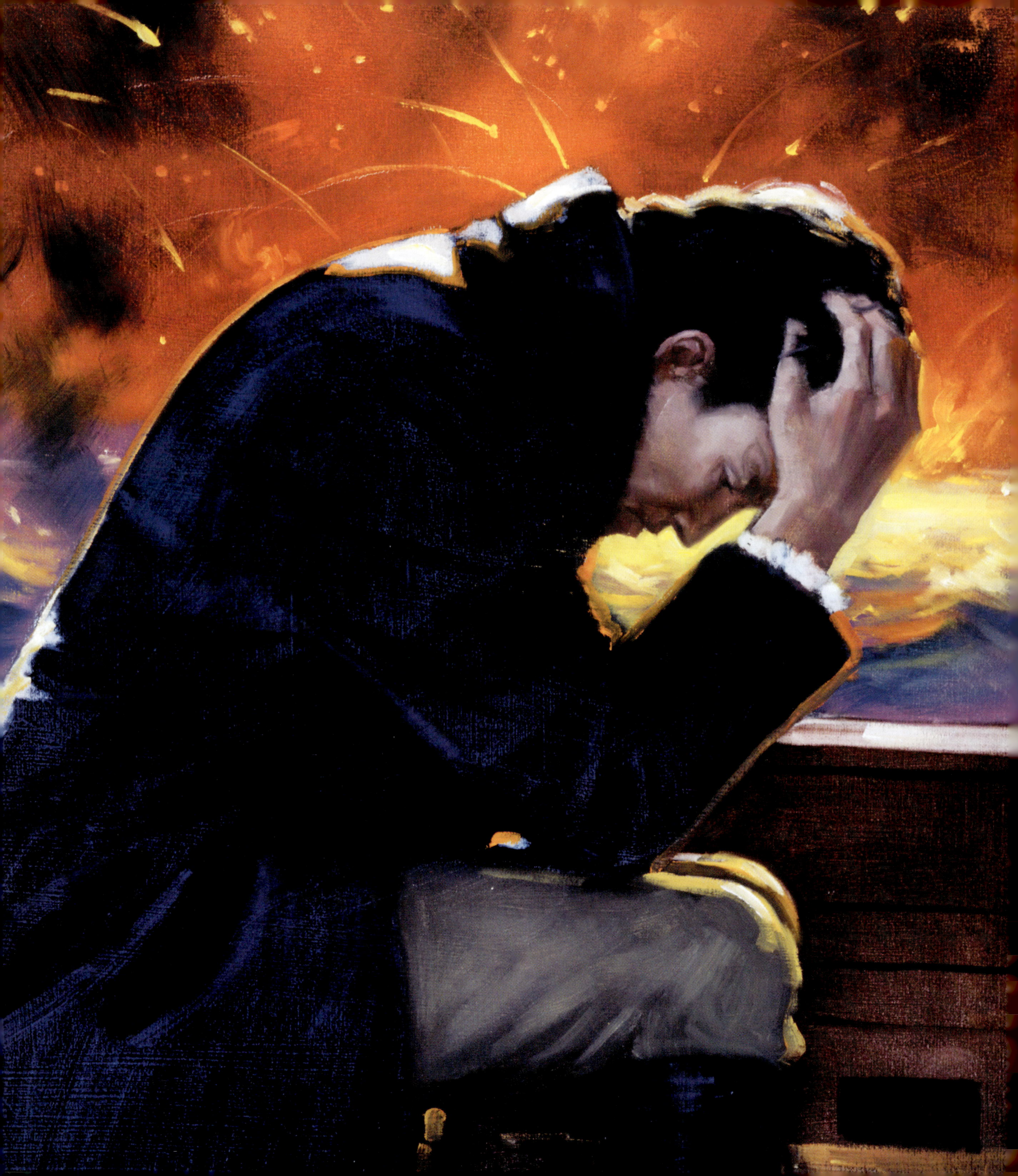

Francis thought that he understood the price of freedom, and he appreciated the sacrifice of men like George Washington and his father, but now he knew that he had never fully understood. There were men – fellow Americans – dying within the walls of Fort McHenry. And then there would be the women and children in Baltimore.

"If only I could warn them!" Francis put his head in his hands in anguish. There was nothing he could do but pray for God's divine protection.

The bombing continued well into the night. Nothing changed until nearly two o'clock in the morning.

"Francis," Colonel Skinner whispered through the damp night air. "Listen; do you hear the sound of oars breaking the water? I fear they are rowing men to shore in skiffs."

"They mean to attack the fort by foot!" Francis said. "They must feel that her walls are badly damaged…that she can no longer defend …" Francis' words faded into the night. The cheers of the enemy filled the air – so sure were they of victory.

"Their yells chill the blood in my veins and pierce my patriotic heart like a dagger," he said. Francis strained to see through the darkness.

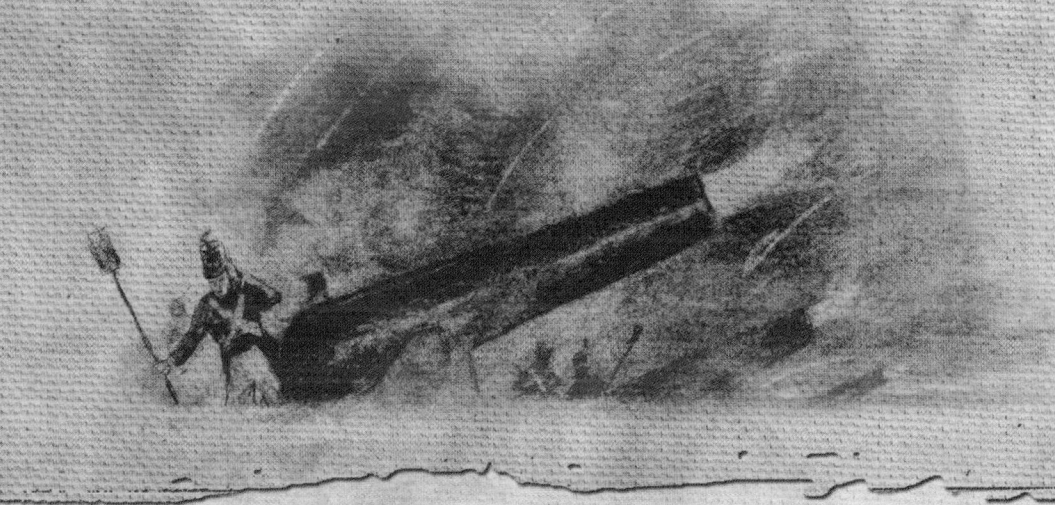

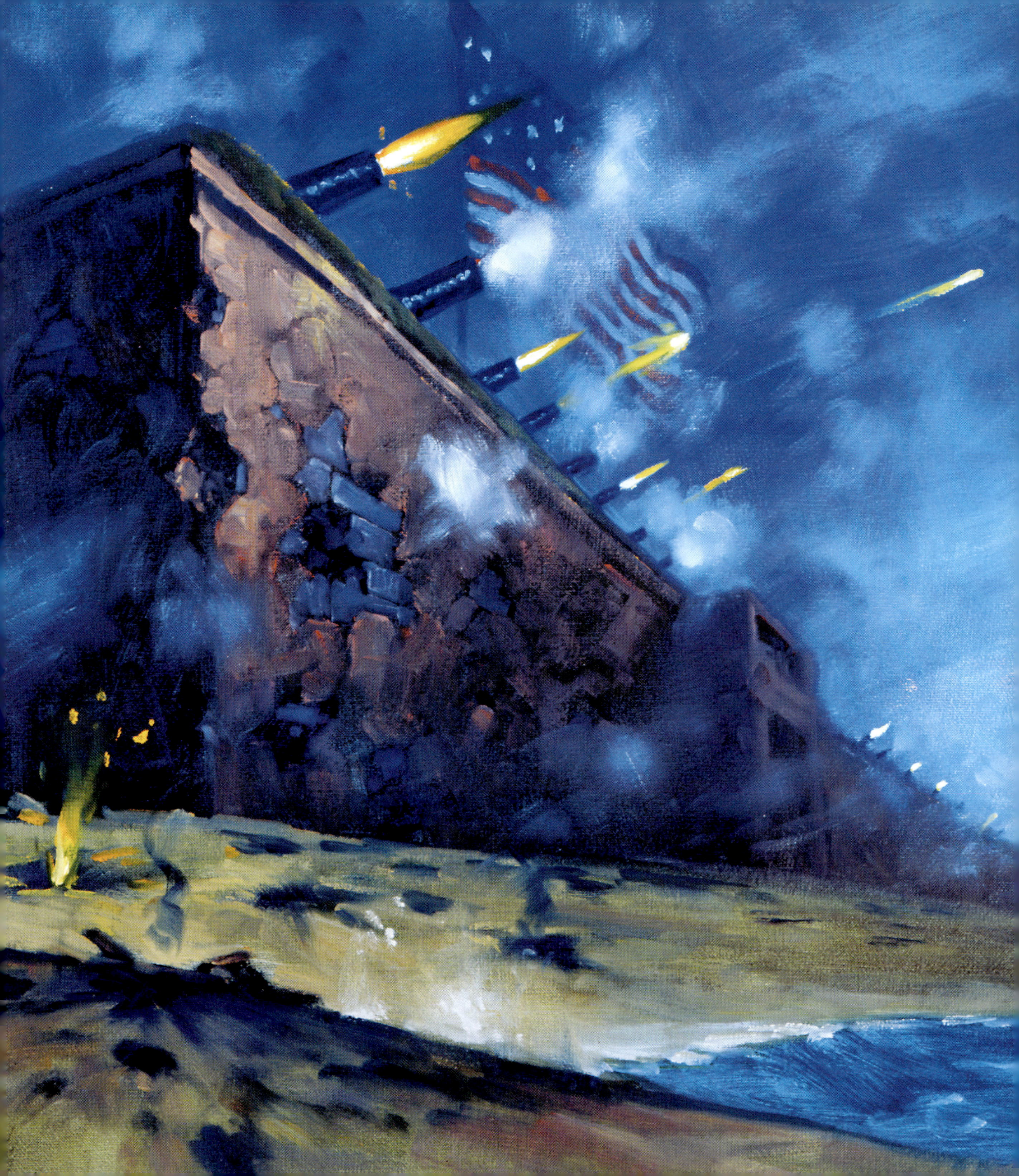

All at once, Fort McHenry opened full fire on the approaching British. The heavy artillery was unlike anything he had ever witnessed.

"Look!" Francis cried. "The sky is glowing like an angry sea of fire. Fort McHenry is fighting back. She still stands! I can see the flag through the glow of the bombs bursting in air."

The cannon blasts were so frequent that the waters in the harbor lashed and pitched in the wake of the explosions. Their little vessel rode and tossed as if in a winter storm. Francis could hear the shrieks and groans of the wounded and dying.

"What does it mean?" Francis cried, as he struggled to see the shoreline and maintain his balance on the tossing deck. "Are they the cries of our men or the British?"

The horrible scene and screams of terror lasted for more than an hour. Suddenly, all was still. Nothing disrupted the night air except the sound of the waves lapping against the side of their vessel. Even the rain had stopped. Fort Mc Henry lay as still as a graveyard. Had she fallen?

For several hours, the only noise that stole through the darkness was the sound of Francis Scott Key's heavy footsteps as he paced the deck. The others had gone to bed, but he could not sleep – the awful silence was too much to bear.

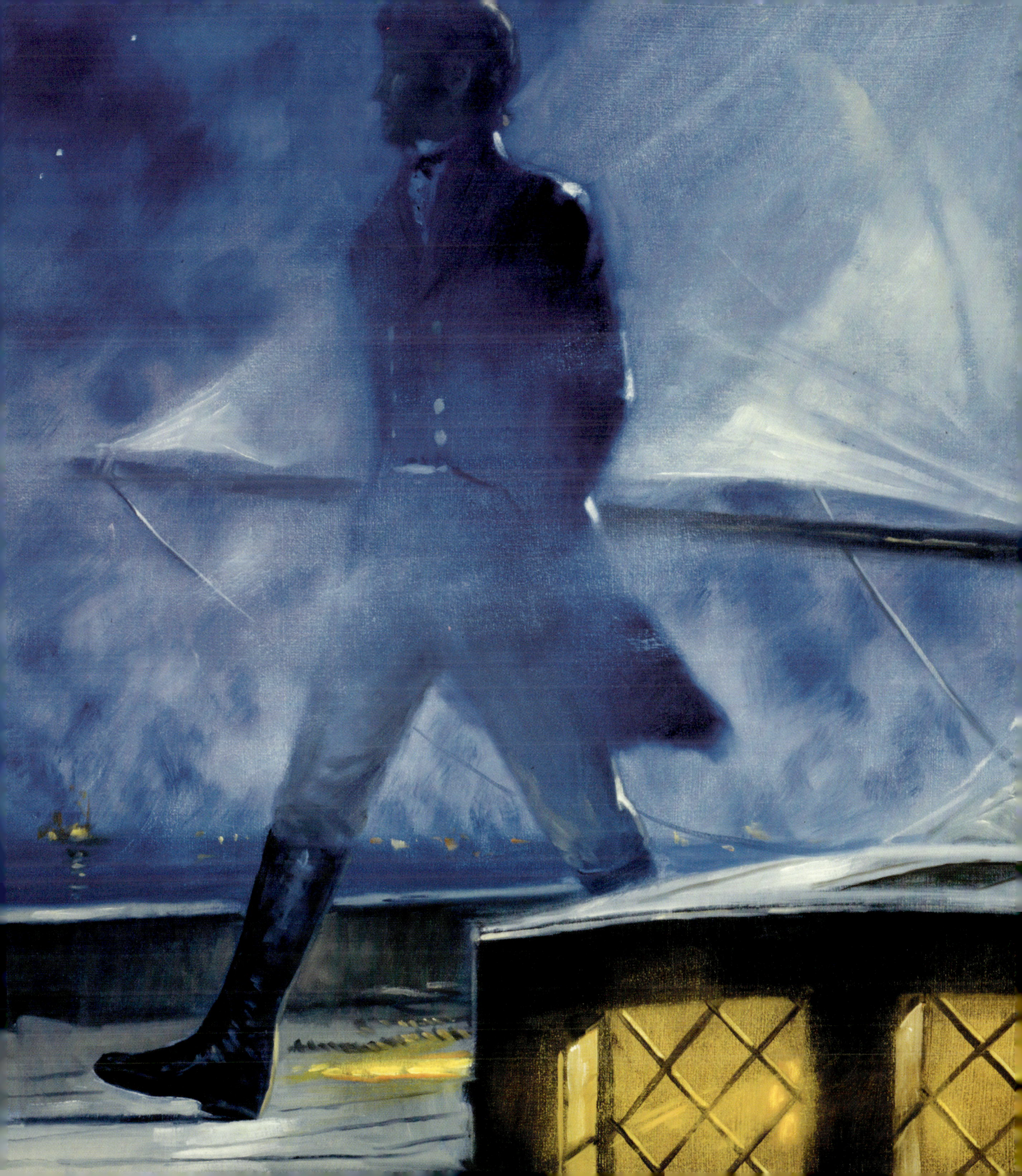

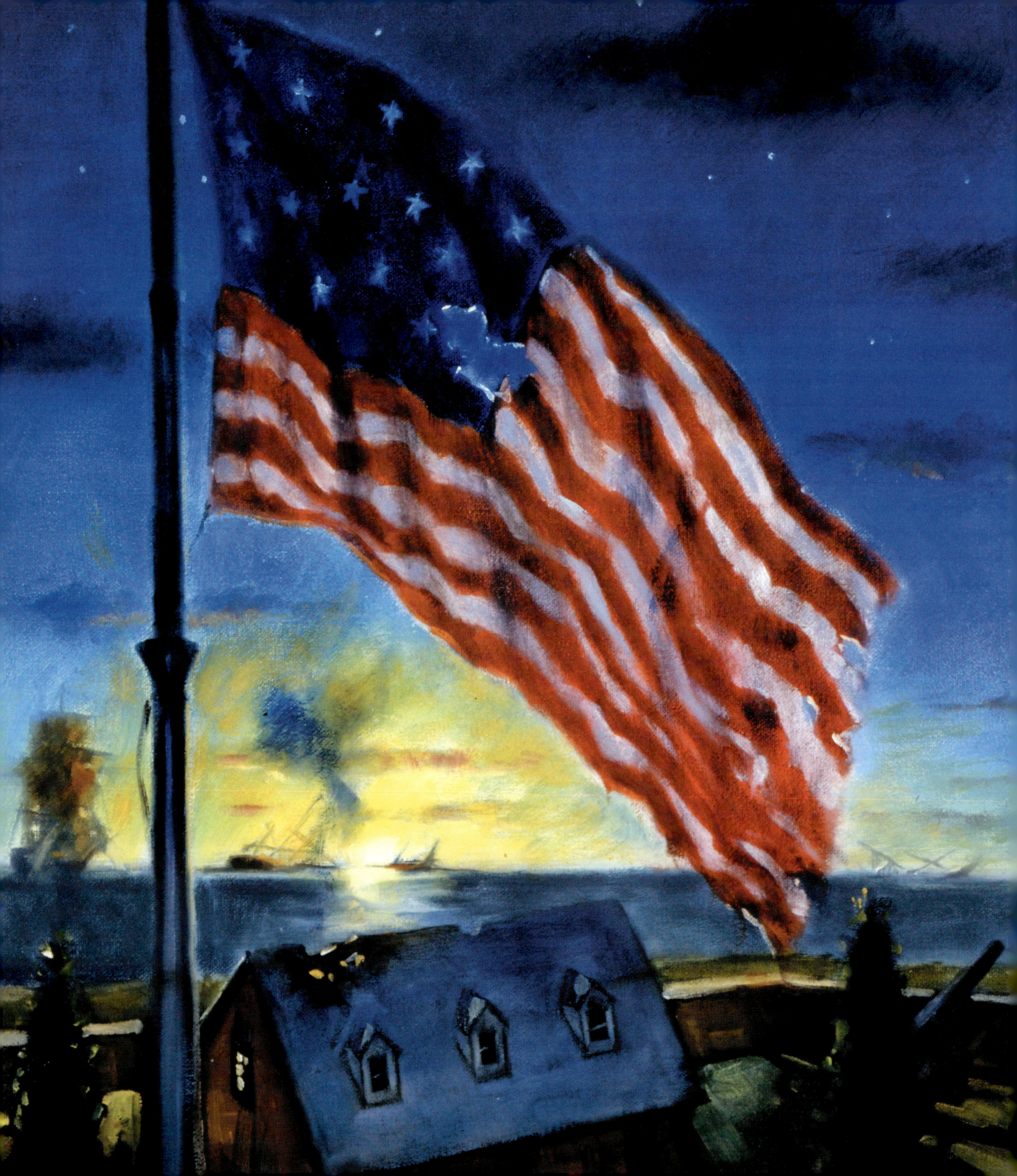

At first, Francis could only see dark fog and smoke though his spyglass, but soon the morning sun pierced its gleaming rays through the darkness. A mixture of hope and fear ran through his veins. Gradually, a smile broke across Francis' tense facial features.

"I see it! Our flag is still there!" Francis cried. He looked toward heaven and unashamed tears streamed down his face. "Providence has protected our heaven-rescued land."

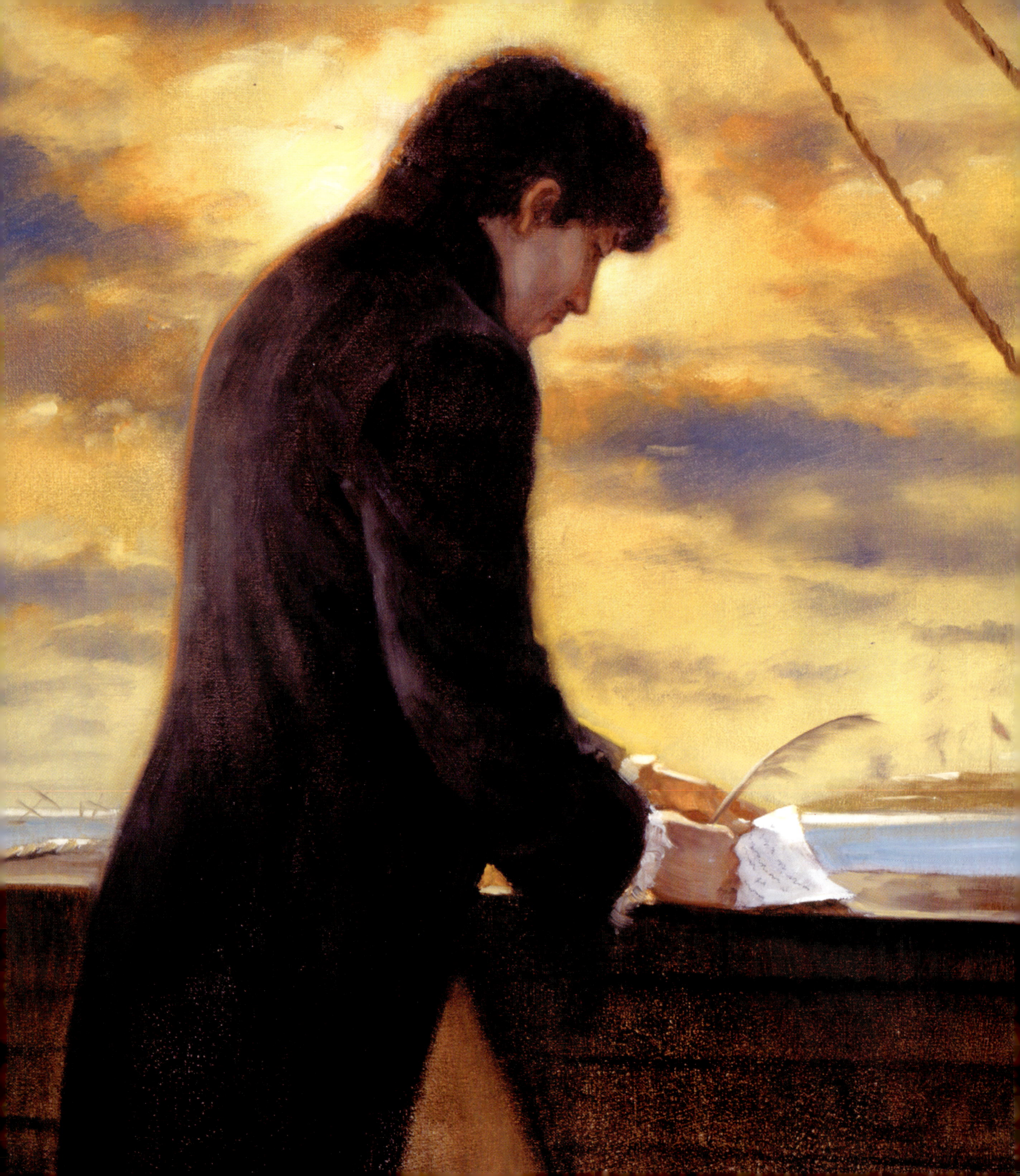

There was much celebration on their little vessel that morning, but Francis drew away. He quickly secured a quill pen and ink from below deck and pulled out a letter he carried in his back pocket. On the envelope, he wrote down his thoughts. He never wanted to forget the emotion he felt that glorious morning. Never would he forget the price of freedom!

The Star Spangled Banner

Oh, say can you see, by the dawn's early light,
What so proudly we hailed at the twilight's last gleaming?
Whose broad stripes and bright stars, through the perilous fight,
O'er the ramparts we watched, were so gallantly streaming?
And the rockets' red glare, the bombs bursting in air,
Gave proof through the night that our flag was still there.
O say, does that star-spangled banner yet wave
O'er the land of the free and the home of the brave?

On the shore, dimly seen through the mists of the deep,
Where the foe's haughty host in dread silence reposes,
What is that which the breeze, o'er the towering steep,
As it fitfully blows, now conceals, now discloses?
Now it catches the gleam of the morning's first beam,
In full glory reflected now shines on the stream:
'Tis the star-spangled banner! O long may it wave
O'er the land of the free and the home of the brave.

And where is that band who so vauntingly swore
That the havoc of war and the battle's confusion
A home and a country should leave us no more?
Their blood has wiped out their foul footstep's pollution.
No refuge could save the hireling and slave
From the terror of flight, or the gloom of the grave:
And the star-spangled banner in triumph doth wave
O'er the land of the free and the home of the brave.

Oh! thus be it ever, when freemen shall stand
Between their loved homes and the war's desolation!
Blest with victory and peace, may the heaven-rescued land
Praise the Power that hath made and preserved us a nation.
Then conquer we must, when our cause it is just,
And this be our motto: "In God is our trust."
And the star-spangled banner in triumph shall wave
O'er the land of the free and the home of the brave!

by Francis Scott Key

Our National Anthem

Francis Scott Key wrote "The Star-Spangled Banner" directly after the battle of Fort McHenry on September 14, 1814.

Within days the poem was published in the *Baltimore Patriot* newspaper under the title "The Defense of Fort McHenry" and was quickly circulated throughout the city and surrounding countryside. Soon the poem was sung to the tune of "Anacreon in Heaven" and titled "The Star-Spangled Banner."

The new song spread rapidly, reaching all the way to the streets of New Orleans within weeks of publication. Though the song was widely known and immediately popular, "The Star-Spangled Banner" did not officially become our national anthem until March 3, 1931.

Additional Works
by
TRACY MICHELE LEININGER

Alone Yet Not Alone
The Story of Barbara & Regina Leininger

Unfading Beauty
The Story of Dolley Madison

Nothing Can Separate Us
The Story of Nan Harper

A Light Kindled
The Story of Priscilla Mullins

The Land Beyond the Setting Sun
The Story of Sacagawea

TO ORDER, CONTACT:

HIS SEASONS®

8122 Datapoint Drive
Suite 1000
San Antonio, TX 78229
(210) 490-2101
www.hisseasons.com